Bungee Jump

Pam Withers

orca currents

ORCA BOOK PUBLISHERS

Library and Archives Canada Cataloguing in Publication

Withers, Pam, author
Bungee jump / Pam Withers.
(Orca currents)

Issued in print and electronic formats.
ISBN 978-1-4598-1216-1 (paperback).—ISBN 978-1-4598-1217-8 (pdf).—
ISBN 978-1-4598-1218-5 (epub)

I. Title. II. Series: Orca currents
PS8595.I8453B86 2016 jC813'.6 C2016-900452-X
C2016-900453-8

First published in the United States, 2016
Library of Congress Control Number: 2016931869

Summary: In this high-interest novel for middle readers, thirteen-year-old Chris is setting up a commercial bungee jump on a historical island that was once the site of a hospital for children with leprosy.

Orca Book Publishers is dedicated to preserving the environment and has printed this book on Forest Stewardship Council® certified paper.

Orca Book Publishers gratefully acknowledges the support for its publishing programs provided by the following agencies: the Government of Canada through the Canada Book Fund and the Canada Council for the Arts,and the Province of British Columbia through the BC Arts Council and the Book Publishing Tax Credit.

Cover photography by Getty Images
Author photo by Cory Permack

ORCA BOOK PUBLISHERS
www.orcabook.com

Printed and bound in Canada.

19 18 17 16 • 4 3 2 1

Chapter One

My younger sister, Caitlin, wanted to visit the island one last time before the engineer moved onto it. She wanted to climb through the old rusty pipe to get there. Both the island and pipe are rumored to be haunted.

I hate dark, enclosed spaces. When I was little I got trapped for an hour in a closet, playing hide-and-seek.

And I'm not crazy about ghosts. Not that I believe in ghosts. What thirteen-year-old guy does? So I won't crawl through dark pipes, but I'm not going to let my eleven-year-old sister do this alone.

"Fog's really thick, Chris," Caitlin says as we reach the top of the bluff.

"Thick enough we can't see our house," I say, glancing down the hill behind us. "That's a good thing. Means Mom and Dad can't see us." The pipe is dry inside and just big enough to crawl through. Originally, the pipe was installed to carry water to a power station on the island. But no one ever built the station. Instead, someone built a hospital for children with leprosy.

The hospital was shut down seventy years ago. My grandfather bought the island cheap, because of its history. He upgraded the pipe just before he died, but until recently Dad had never found a use for it. We use the land on the peninsula for a tree farm that doesn't make much money, but the island and the pipe have gone unused for years.

Suspended fifteen stories above Misty Passage, the pipe is encased in crisscrossed steel supports. It's like a high bridge without walkway or railings. Mom and Dad won't let us go near it.

Like that has ever stopped us. We've been using the pipe to get to the island for years. Caitlin crawls through. I crawl along the top, like we are doing now.

I hear a muffled "Ouch!" and know Caitlin has hit her head on the boxlike hatch that hangs down from the middle. Again.

"Can't wait for the bungee jump to be built," Caitlin says as she emerges from the pipe on the island.

"Me too," I agree, trying to picture a thick rope dangling from a sparkling new steel platform above the pipe. "And I get to see a real engineer at work."

"Yeah, geek, he'll be asking you for your expertise for sure." My sister laughs. "More important, Dad says it'll bring us real money."

"Mmm." The only trouble is, I know Dad spent way too much money on the plans, the engineer and materials.

The bungee jump was my idea. Caitlin and I got to go on one in Oregon during spring break. There was a huge lineup for it, and the site was nowhere near as cool as our property. It took Dad a while to come around to the notion that a bungee jump could make money on our pipe bridge, but he eventually decided to have plans drawn up. Then he arranged to hire an engineer-contractor to build it. That guy will be arriving any day now.

"Hope no one tells the contractor that the island has ghosts," I joke. Local legend claims that the island is haunted by the ghosts of the leper children who died there. And of the doctor who fell—or jumped—from the pipe when he got the disease. Sometimes I hear creepy noises near the pipe or island.

We slide down the muddy path toward the ruins of the hospital. It's invisible in the fog. I tell myself no spooks are hiding out in the soupy cloud.

"Mrs. Dubin says there were fifty children here before the hospital closed," I say. I run my hands along the mossy top of a tumbledown wall.

"Mrs. Dubin is annoying," Caitlin says. "What is she, like, a hundred?" My sister doesn't like the old lady who runs our school library. It's true that she's moody, but she's usually friendly to me. Anyway, I like hearing her stories about our hick town in the old days.

"She told me she was born the year the hospital got shut down," I say. "So she's seventy. And she knows a lot about Hospital Island."

"Like what?" Caitlin is winding through the corridors of the old place. She pokes her head into rooms where pieces of ceiling have fallen onto rusty bedsprings.

"The real name of the island is Thorn Island. But the locals started calling it Hospital Island when the hospital was built." I kick a loose brick on the floor, which sends up plumes of dust. "This place only ran for ten years."

"I knew that." Caitlin sniffs and runs her hand through a giant cobweb.

"One doctor and one nurse worked here—"

"What happened to the nurse?" Caitlin asks.

"Disappeared after the doctor jumped."

"Where did the kids go then?"

"To some other leper hospital in California."

"What else?" Caitlin asks, moving into a different wing.

"The story about the cash box is baloney. Made up."

Caitlin shrugs. "Makes a good story. Might be true. Evil doctor rips off all the money meant to feed the children and buy medicine—"

"—and buries it somewhere on the island, never yet found," I finish for her. "Made up. False."

"If you believe old Dubin," says Caitlin.

"Why would she lie about that?" I ask.

"I don't know," says Caitlin. "She's a crank. You know she hates our bungee-jump idea."

"Yeah. She doesn't want history disturbed," I say. "And I kind of get that." I don't know why I'm defending the old librarian.

"Nah, it's 'cause she's too old to bounce on a bungee-jump rope. She's jealous of us." Caitlin and I both laugh at that.

"Shhh." I hold up my hand. "Hear something?"

We go dead silent. I hear lapping water and two faint voices. I shudder. Phantoms of the doctor and leper kids?

We move out of the hospital ruins and stand onshore. Caitlin leans into me. I don't like that she's scared too.

Smack! A tall dark figure holding a noose leaps from the water and knocks me down. Then starts howling.

I scream and flee into the frigid channel, ready to swim home. But the cold instantly gives me corpse legs.

As I back up, there's deep laughter. A strange man leans down and pulls me aboard a barge.

"That was just Dad," Caitlin calls out, giggling. "He was landing with the rope to tie up the boat, silly."

"Chris," says Dad from shore, "sorry to knock you over. But why'd you head into the water? This here's Gord Plant, our engineer, by the way."

Gord, a skinny man with a mop of red hair, has hold of my jacket. He's laughing a belly laugh. "I thought you were going to do a polar-bear swim there for a second. Sure soaked your jeans and shoes, eh? Did you think we were ghosts?"

"What're you doing on the island anyway?" Dad asks, looking from Caitlin to me. "You'd better not have come by the pipe, or you're both grounded."

"Aww, give 'em a break, Buzz," Gord says. "Good to meet you, Chris and Caitlin. Chris, I'll fetch a towel for you from the trailer."

That's when I see that the barge I'm on is hooked up to a towboat Dad was driving. Tied securely on the barge is a scruffy little trailer. Gord's home during the platform construction.

"H-h-hi," I say, my burning face warming me. I drip onto the barge deck amid the noise of three people laughing at me once again. "Welcome to Hospital Island."

Chapter Two

It's lunchtime when I know Caitlin has said something at school about last night.

Two guys walk by with smirks. "Quick! Run into the water! They're after you!"

Ten minutes later, Caitlin's friends Bella and Anya cruise by, waving their arms and chanting like ghosts. "Owoooo! Ooooo! Boo!"

In the lunchroom half the school is walking stiffly, imitating zombies, then falling down and cracking up. Even my friend Tom and some of our gang have smeared their faces with paint.

"Tom, not you too," I say. "Knock it off."

"Aww, Chris, we're just having a little fun."

Right. I offer a weak smile and sit down next to Tom. We chat for a while as we eat our sandwiches. Some of our other friends join us, done with the teasing.

But other students keep making digs as they pass our table.

"Sorry, guys," I finally say. "I'm getting out of here."

Tom grins like he understands. So I flee down the hall, my running shoes squeaking on the polished floor.

"Chris!" I crash into Mrs. Dubin. With terrible timing, she has just stepped out of the library. She wags a knobby finger in my face. "No running in the halls." Then her face softens. "Got some new books in on leprosy. For that school report. Hope you have a strong stomach. Shows people with claws for hands and horrible face sores."

"Uh, thanks, Mrs. Dubin. Later," I say.

I dodge past her and duck into the science room. No one's in here. I slump into a desk. The students mocking me are jerks. All I did was wade into the water. How dare Caitlin say anything when she was just as spooked!

"Hey there, Chris." A pair of polished brown shoes and the hem of a white lab coat move into view.

I sit up straight. "Um, hi, Mr. Roth."

"Stopped in to work on your science-fair project during lunch hour? It's coming along nicely."

"Yeah." I move hurriedly to my two-foot-wide suspension-bridge model.

It sits on a counter between other kids' less ambitious projects.

"You're a natural-born engineer, Chris. I'm impressed."

I flush but lift my face and smile. "That's what I want to be."

"I've no doubt."

He taps the suspender cables on my bridge model. "Perfect stiffness and aerodynamic profiling. This will last under high winds."

"Thanks. I got the stainless-steel wire in the hardware store."

"You achieved the balance between dead load, live load and dynamic load right." This is a big compliment. It means I managed to counterbalance the bridge weight, traffic weight and the bridge's ability to cope with wind and earthquakes.

"The engineer for our bungee jump just got here," I say.

"Excellent. You'll learn a lot from him if he lets you hang around while he's working."

I nod. It's what I'm hoping.

"Did I tell you I studied to be a structural engineer before I decided to be a teacher instead?"

"Yup."

"I could be building bridges now instead of correcting papers," he muses.

"Thanks for helping me with my bridge."

He pats it. "The whole town's waiting for your bungee jump to open. It'll be the best entertainment in town."

"Got that right," I agree. I get saved from further conversation and zombie encounters by the bell.

"Traitor," I say accusingly to Caitlin after the day's final bell. She has just caught up to me on my way out of school.

"I only told one person," she insists.

"Bella, I bet. She has a big mouth." I pick up my pace, so Caitlin has to jog to keep up.

"I'm sorry—" she starts.

"Ahoyyyy there! You two!"

The bellowing voice comes from Misty Passage. We've just turned onto the path along it.

"It's that crazy fisherman," Caitlin whispers.

"He's not crazy. Just not friendly. Ignore him," I advise her.

"Ahoyyyy there! You two!"

I look at the tall barrel-chested man in the wooden rowboat. He's standing up, oars trailing as he shakes his fists at us.

"Stop! I wanna talk to you!" he shouts.

"What do you want?" I ask. Caitlin slams into me as I stop on the path.

"You get that man off the island!" he commands, eyes narrowed.

"What man?" I play along.

"The one with the trailer! You get him off!"

"Or what? It's *our* island!" I toss back.

The fisherman looks so startled that his body tilts toward shore. He is on the brink of tumbling in. Caitlin grabs my arm like she wants us to run.

"It's not yours. It's *theirs*!" he thunders. "Better watch out if they wake up!" The fists are punching the air again.

I'm tempted to laugh, but he seems mad enough as it is. I calculate how fast he could row to shore and sprint after us before I wave and turn away. I head for home at an unhurried pace. Caitlin is on my heels.

I have a bad feeling as we walk through the front door. Dad and Mom are sitting serious-faced on the sofa. Dad is comforting Mom, who has red eyes.

"Chris, Caitlin," he says in a quiet tone as we enter.

"What's up?" I ask, looking from one to the other.

"I've been offered a great new job," he says. "But it means I have to move to the city for a little while. I start next week."

"Huh? Why?" we ask in unison.

"We really need the money."

Mom turns away to wipe her eyes, then faces us. "It won't be for long, kids. We'll be okay."

Dad walks over and puts his hand on my shoulder. "Chris…"

Sadness and anger well up. He hasn't asked us if he can disappear off to the city. Or given us any warning.

"You really have to?" I challenge.

Caitlin throws her arms around Dad like she can stop him. Mom is biting her lower lip.

We're losing Dad all because he has done a lousy job of managing the tree farm, I think. Or maybe because he agreed to pay this Gord guy too much. No, wait, he told me Gord was way cheaper than other engineers who'd applied. Lots of good that did.

We talk, we hug, we finally eat supper together. When I go to bed, I punch a pillow so hard that feathers fly.

Chapter Three

"Chris!" Mom calls after breakfast a week later. "Dad's on the phone."

I finish loading my books into my backpack. "Hi, Dad!"

"Chris, son! Good to hear your voice."

"How's work in the city?"

"It's tough," he says cheerfully. "But it sure pays well."

I stay quiet. I'm not about to tell him how glum we are without him. Or how Mom, Caitlin and I are working ourselves to exhaustion every day chopping firewood. He usually did most of that.

"How's the bungee jump looking?"

I brighten. "He's patched the pipe and is painting it. I helped. And a pile of steel supports has arrived. For the gridwork upgrade."

"That's super. Two engineers at work together," Dad jokes. "Well, that brings me to what I want to ask you."

I wait.

"While I'm not there, Chris, I need you to be my man, okay? Keep an eye on Gord. Make sure the project goes like it's supposed to. Supervise him and report the progress to me."

Me, in charge of an engineer? I'm just a kid! "Um, okay," I say.

Dad's voice lowers. "That bungee jump is our future, Chris. Without it, we and the farm go down. I need you."

"When are you coming home, Dad?"

He sighs. "Soon as I can, Chris."

"Okay. Got to go to school now. Bye." I want to say, *I miss you*, or ask why he got us into money problems or tell him to come home now. Instead, I hand the phone to Mom and run out the front door.

"Chris, wait!" Caitlin chases after me.

I wait just long enough for her to catch up.

"Science-fair results today," she reminds me.

"Uh-huh." My heart beats faster as I spot the big Science Fair banner over the school's front door.

We enter the gym. There's a ton of students and parents. They hover over and gawk at the dozens of displays on tables around the room. I attempt to elbow my way over to mine, where the thickest gathering is.

"Here he is!" I hear Mr. Roth's voice. People turn, and the crowd parts to let me through.

My eyes fix on my bridge. It's just like when I turned it in—slim pillars, vertical suspender cables, tons of tiny wires and cables and plates. Except for the blue ribbon hung on it.

"Congratulations!" Friends punch me in the shoulder, smiling at me. They say things like, "Way to go" and "Knew you'd do something great."

"You rock!" says Tom.

"It's amazing," crows Bella.

Then suddenly everyone's pressing around it. They ask me questions. I answer them all. After all the research I had to do to make the model, I know a lot about bridge construction.

"It certainly deserved to win first place!" Mr. Roth says, and I turn pink.

"All it's missing is a bungee-jump rope!" Anya says. The next thing I know, the kids are crowding around Caitlin and me to ask about the bungee jump.

"How long will the rope be?"

"Can you go on it upside down?"

"When is it opening?"

"How much will it cost?"

"Wow, I can't wait!"

By the time the bell rings, I'm standing with my head held high. And thinking maybe the bungee jump really will save our tree farm.

Chapter Four

"Chris!" Gord greets me as I arrive panting from climbing the bluff. He places his measuring tape back into his tool belt and plops down on the newly painted pipe. "Home from school already? No homework?"

That probably means I bug him too much. But hey, nothing can keep me away. It's cool watching him work.

I really like seeing the trestle part (steel beams around the pipe) getting repaired. And I especially like asking Gord questions.

Gord studies the plans he keeps in a red binder. He flips pages back and forth like he's confused about something. He wipes sweat from his neck.

"You have to calculate for loading and size, right?" I ask.

"Of course," he says, frowning.

"My science teacher says the welding is the most important part." Welding, of course, is joining metal pieces together—fusing and hammering them.

"Is that so?" His eyes are still on the plans.

"When does the boom crane come to put in the catwalk?" I ask.

"The what? Oh. Soon, Chris."

"And what's the catwalk made of?"

"Steel mesh. Twenty inches wide."

"My science teacher says you'll get a shop to pre-make it in pieces. Then you'll use the crane to put them together."

"Uh-huh."

"I can't wait till the platform is on. Can I see the plans again, please?"

Gord slams the binder closed and hands it to me.

"Something wrong?" I ask. I hope he's not going to send me away. He hasn't yet. I'm the boss's son, after all. Or the boss, if you read Dad's most recent letter to Gord. It's in my jeans pocket, ready to deliver to him.

"Just trying to make sense of some stuff."

"Oh." I turn back to the binder.

The final drawing shows the fixed-up pipe surrounded by stronger steel casing. The repaired frame resembles a long, airy boxcar with steel Xs on the top, bottom and sides. Like a freight-train section frozen midair over the channel, carrying the pipe.

On top is a narrow walkway with sturdy railings. That's the catwalk. Halfway across the bridge, the catwalk opens onto a platform. It sticks out over the water, a sort of topless metal cage with a gate. Under the cage is the bungee-jump anchor and winch. (A winch is machinery that pulls things up.) Whoever steps through the gate is on a plank like a diving board.

Two diagonal railings support the jump-off point like it's a drawbridge about to be pulled up. Giant red foot-prints are painted on the end of the board to show where the jumper stands before leaping.

The jump master—that's the guy in charge of checking jumpers' equipment before saying, "Go!"—will stand inside the cage.

"So the platform is eight by eight feet," I muse. "Whoa, can you imagine standing on it, ready to jump 150 feet down into—?"

"*Ahoyyy up there!*"

"Oh no, not him again," Gord mumbles.

"*Ahoyyy down there!*" I dare to shout to the rowboat. "That's Craven, the fisherman," I tell Gord. "He's grumpy but harmless. You can ignore him."

"The more I ignore him, the more he bugs me," Gord says.

"You tell her to stay off the island!" Craven instructs me.

"Who?" I respond impatiently.

"She's disturbing them."

"Who's disturbing whom?"

"You're disturbing us!" Gord inserts for good measure.

Craven shakes his head like we're the troublesome ones. "Your sister is bothering the children!"

I stand up so fast I almost fall off the pipe.

"Is Caitlin on Hospital Island? By herself? Now?"

"She's on Thorn Island. She was bothering the children. They got mad."

"Where's Thorn Island, and what children?" Gord asks me. He pauses from scribbling numbers on the plans.

"Thorn Island is what Hospital Island used to be called. And he's talking about the leper children. I mean, the ghosts of the leper children." I attempt a chuckle, but it comes out like a hiccupy cough. "Sorry, Gord. Gotta go. But Dad asked me to give this to you."

Gord accepts the envelope and stares at me. I scramble up and start crawling. My knees are on the pipe. My hands are on the cagelike structure around it.

"Hey! That's not safe, Christopher Bigg!" Gord calls out to me. "You get down right now. Safer to crawl *through* if you have to go across, you know."

"Caitlin crawls through. I crawl on top," I inform him. Halfway across, while crawling over the hatch, I glance down at Craven. He scowls upward.

"*You're* in charge?" Gord shouts suddenly, waving the letter he has just opened. "A thirteen-year-old is my boss?" He laughs like it's the best joke he has heard all day. "Now I've heard everything!"

I should answer back, but I know I have to check on my sister. My knees go into high gear. I move like a jockey on a racehorse. When I reach solid ground, I sprint downhill. Into the hospital ruins, down the corridors. I zigzag from one cruddy room to another, trying to locate a faint shouting.

"Chris! Someone! *Heeeelp!*" comes her muffled voice. I enter a room that ages ago must have been tiled from ceiling to floor. Now the squares of ceramic are covered in filth. Half the pieces are missing. Rusty pipes run down the walls. Piles of moldy leaves mush underfoot.

"*Heeelp* me!" Banging is coming from under a big rotted square of heavy wood. It must have fallen from where it was leaning against the wall.

I grab hold and try to lift it. It won't budge. Grunting, I try again. This time it comes up. "Quick!" I urge my dirt-covered sister as she pokes her tear-stained face up from some kind of former hot tub. "Get out before I lose my grip."

She bolts free like a rabbit out of a hole. The second she's clear, I let go, and the wood comes crashing down again. It cracks and sends dust flying.

I'm sneezing. Caitlin clings to me.

"What are you doing here? What happened?" I ask.

"Exploring this old pool. I was wiping dirt off the tiles. Underneath, it's kind of pretty. There are lots of colors and designs."

"And the leper children didn't like you here. So they crashed the board down and trapped you," I say dryly.

Caitlin's eyes grow big. "D-d-do you really think so?" She clutches me harder and looks around the room.

"Of course not. But that's what Craven told me."

"How'd he know I—?"

"Probably got out of his boat and saw you. I've seen him using the outhouse on the island before. Then rowed out to tell me. Anyway, it's not safe here. Especially by yourself. If Dad knew, he'd—"

"Yeah, well, he's not here. And you're not Dad. And you're never around to play with anymore. All you care about is Gord and that stupid—"

"It's not stupid, Caitlin. And it's my job to make sure Gord is doing it right."

At this, she peels herself away and crosses her arms. The glare on her filthy face is enough to scare away a roomful of ghosts.

"Yeah, right," she huffs.

"Did you hear any noise before that board came down?"

Caitlin uncrosses her arms and looks around warily. "I don't think so."

"So it came down all by itself?"

"I guess."

"'Cause if someone is trying to scare you, they'll be sorry. No one messes with the Bigg family!" I say it loud enough for trespassers, vandals, jokers and ghosts to hear.

Chapter Five

I'm in the school library, looking at books on leprosy. Mrs. Dubin was right. The people in the photos and drawings are gross. Weird lumps and sores all over their bodies, toes and fingers like scarecrow sticks.

"No wonder people used to dump them on islands. Didn't want anyone else to catch the disease," I say as she wanders up and peers over my shoulder.

"That was before they knew leprosy wasn't very contagious after all," Mrs. Dubin says.

"They are kind of ugly," I muse. I turn pages that show medieval drawings. I see lepers slumped on village streets, collecting coins.

"Yes, the muscle weakness caused by the disease made their bodies crooked. That's also why their toes and fingers shrank. And the sores didn't help. People were deathly afraid of them. Those who helped sometimes caught the disease. There weren't plastic gloves and mouth masks then."

"So the doctor and nurse who helped leper children on Hospital Island were really brave, right?"

"Thorn Island," she corrects me. Then she straightens, and her smile lights her face. "Brave and generous, Chris. Heroes, I'd say."

"Except then the doctor got the disease and—"

"No one really knows what happened to him," she interrupts with a frown.

"That story about him stealing and hiding the money. What do you think?"

"I think you should stick to your school report," she snaps.

Whoa, what'd she have for breakfast?

"And you should never, ever visit Thorn Island. It disturbs the children's spirits."

"Mmmm," I reply.

She shuffles away. I look from the library book to my empty notebook page. I sigh and read more. Then I start writing so fast that my hand cramps:

Leprosy (Hansen's disease)

Symptoms: sores, rashes and lumps all over the body. (Yuck!) Especially on eyes, nose, ears, hands and feet. Numbness and weak muscles that make toes and fingers shrink. Like they've fallen off or something. If they don't get medicine, lepers eventually can't walk, go blind and die. Children catch leprosy easier than adults.

Where lepers lived: in leper colonies, places that other people wouldn't visit. Especially islands. Until about seventy-five years ago. Including ~~Hospital~~ Thorn Island.

History: Leprosy was considered incurable and very contagious. So lepers were banned and avoided. Only brave doctors, priests and monks would try to help them.

Cause: a germ

Cure: discovered in 1982 (whew!)

Brrrrng!

All right, the bell! Time's up, and I'm out of here to play basketball with my friends before I head home.

"Gord's not on the pipe," Caitlin reports when I get home.

"He should be," I say.

"You going to make him?" She smiles. "He's on Hospital Island with some weird tool, wandering around like he's lost something."

"Let's get the boat and go see."

Minutes later I'm rowing our family dinghy over, ready to *disturb the children's spirits* if I have to. I need to make sure Gord earns the money our family is paying him.

The engineer doesn't notice us as we pull to shore.

"See?" Caitlin whispers.

He's bent over a metal rod with a circle of black metal on the end, hovering a few inches from the ground. He is wandering in circles, eyes intent on the device. "What's that?" I wonder aloud.

Caitlin shrugs. "I dunno, but I don't think it has anything to do with the bungee jump."

I lift the oars out of the water, and we tie up the boat. "Hi, Gord!"

He jumps. "Oh, hi, kids. Didn't know you were on the island. This is a metal detector. I lost one of my tools. Hoping it will help me find it."

"Which tool?" I ask.

"Um, screwdriver."

"It's right there on your tool belt."

He looks down. "Well, I'll be! You're right. Thanks, Chris."

"Aren't metal detectors for finding rings and coins and stuff?" Caitlin asks.

"Anything metal," he says.

"Can I try it?" Caitlin asks.

"Um, sure, but—"

"—but right now we have to get to work," I finish for him. "Walk you up to the pipe, Gord?"

His eyebrows slant downward for a moment. Then he nods. "Of course. Got to get ready for that crane tomorrow!"

We work hard for the rest of the afternoon. We clear brush and stuff from the road to make room for the crane and prefab catwalk sections. We're so focused, wc almost forget about Caitlin. She comes rushing up the Hospital Island rise, waving one hand and carrying Gord's metal detector in the other.

"Look what I found!" As she greets us, she lifts something from a pocket before we can answer. "Four bracelets!" She flashes some old copper bangles. "I can wear them in the school play next week!"

"Just like a dancer's bracelets," I say, humoring her.

"Good for you," Gord says less enthusiastically. "But you'll put my detector away carefully in my trailer now, right?"

"You bet!"

"And if you find an old rusty box," he continues, "don't dig it up. Tell me first. It could be dangerous. Could be the leper doctor's tools. They might infect you."

Caitlin's eyes grow large. "Oh. Okay. Thanks, Gord." And with her bracelets jangling, she and the metal detector disappear down the hill to Gord's trailer.

Chapter Six

Mom is wearing a dress and lipstick for a night out to watch the school play. She's making a real effort, even though she has been working long hours.

"I'm so proud you got one of the dancer parts, Caitlin," she says. "And you planned your costume all by yourself."

I've decided not to make fun of my sister's strange outfit—pink tights, sparkly slippers and a too-large silk dress from a charity shop. Around her neck, several bright scarves flutter as she twirls on the path.

"I'm sooo excited!" she says as she shakes her arms to rattle the copper bracelets. "I've found sixteen so far! So I have eight on each arm. Had to polish them, but aren't they shiny now?"

"They're lovely," Mom says, inspecting them. "I feel sorry for the person who lost them."

"Finders keepers," Caitlin says quickly. "No names on them. Just little numbers on the inside."

We deliver my hyped-up sister to the gym's back door. We seat ourselves in the gym. I wave to some friends. The place is full.

The teachers are seated a few rows ahead, close to the front. Mr. Roth turns and waves at me. I wave back. I spot Mrs. Dubin in the row behind him.

I look around. Craven is a few rows behind me. It's nice to see that he gets out of his boat and joins the community sometimes. No sign of Gord. Wonder what he's doing tonight? Resting after the crane and catwalk sections finally came? Maybe playing cards with himself in the trailer? Or wandering around with that stupid metal detector.

"Too bad you didn't audition, Chris," Mom says.

"Not my thing. And it's not like I have the time," I say. "But it's great that Caitlin got a part."

"And her friends Bella and Anya."

"Ladies and gentlemen," the drama teacher says. He's standing in front of the red velvet curtain. "Tonight we are proud to present the play *Tiny Dancers*. Let the show begin!"

We clap, and the older actors come out first. As they recite their parts in flat or overdramatic voices, my mind drifts to the bungee-jump project.

Gord has patched and painted the pipe. He has replaced the steel straps and some gridwork around it. Now the catwalk is here. Tomorrow he starts installing that. Next, the gated platform goes on. Then, maybe in five weeks, the grand opening. If only Dad would finish earning what he needs to and come home to see it.

"The dancers just came out," Mom says, nudging me.

Music has started from some boom box behind the curtain. I sit up straight and try to concentrate. Caitlin, her two friends and three other girls in her grade step into view. The stage lights make their costumes sparkle.

Caitlin is in the middle, grinning like a fairy. She spins, glides and takes over the floor. She's leading the other girls, brimming with confidence. *Way to go, Caitlin!*

In the middle of the number, she dances close to stage's edge, near the teachers. She lifts her arms like a ballerina. Then she does a spin and shakes her wrists. Even people in the back row can probably hear the jingling.

Mom is leaning forward, smiling like crazy. She presses her palms together. One of the teachers rises. Her large body blocks our view. She pushes slowly through a sea of knees to reach the aisle. Lots of people look annoyed.

"Sit back down!" I hear someone shout.

"That's your librarian, isn't it?" Mom asks.

We watch Mrs. Dubin charge up the aisle, finger pointed at Caitlin.

Caitlin stops moving. Her sweaty face reveals confusion and fright.

Mrs. Dubin halts in front of the stage and stares up at Caitlin. Then she collapses onto the floor.

A big commotion starts. Someone shouts, "Call an ambulance! Is there a doctor here?"

Caitlin backs up slowly, as deflated as a punctured balloon. The drama teacher ushers everyone off the stage.

"Poor Caitlin," I mutter.

"Poor Mrs. Dubin," Mom says at the same time.

Chapter Seven

"Hey, Caitlin, how do I spell *adrenaline*?" I'm two years older, but she's sometimes better at spelling. And she needs a distraction from her glum mood this morning.

"Dunno," comes my sister's flat voice. She's lying on the living room sofa. Mom's gone to work already. Caitlin's supposed to clean the house before we head for school. I've already done my chores.

"Don't know or don't care?" I ask. "You're not still moping about the school play, are you? You were great. So what if you didn't get to finish? Everyone saw how awesome you were."

"It's not that."

"They said all Mrs. Dubin did was faint. Wasn't a heart attack or anything," I say. "You never liked her anyway. Now she's off school for a week. So what's the big deal?"

"You didn't see her face."

"I've never seen anyone's face right before they fainted. But get over it already, Caitlin. I need your help writing the bungee-jump website."

She turns toward me with a sour face. "Why do we need a website?"

"To get customers, duh."

"*Adrenaline* has an *e* at the end."

"Thanks."

Caitlin looks over my shoulder at the screen. "Why would including a history of Hospital Island help bring people?" she asks.

I sigh. "It's interesting, Caitlin. There are bungee jumps all over the world. But how many are on a historic island?"

"Historic or haunted? Some of the kids at school say there are really ghosts there."

"You and I know that's baloney. Anyway, it's not going to stop anyone from coming. This is the most exciting thing that has happened to our town in years. All the kids can hardly wait. Are you going to help me or not?"

She shrugs. "Do you think I could get leprosy from touching those copper bracelets?"

"Huh?"

"If they belonged to the leper children from the hospital." She's looking at me with pleading eyes. Sometimes I forget she's only eleven.

"Caitlin, first of all, tons of people have explored that island since the hospital shut down. So the bracelets could've been anyone's."

She waits. I lift my bowl of cereal to my mouth and drain it. "And second, leprosy isn't as contagious as people think."

"Says who?"

"The experts I quoted in my school paper."

"But the doctor got it."

"You can only get it if they sneeze on you or something. Doctors back then didn't have rubber gloves. Or masks to breathe through like today."

She lifts her wrists and studies them like she's looking for leprosy sores. "I just know they belonged to the children."

"How?"

"The look on Mrs. Dubin's face that night. And the numbers on each bracelet. Those bracelets were their identity tags, Chris. That's what I think now."

"You think too much. You can't catch leprosy from old copper bracelets. Trust me."

"Gord says we could get it from the doctor's tools. That's why we're not supposed to touch anything if we find a rusty old box."

"Gord's an engineer, not a doctor. Speaking of Gord, I'd better get up to the bridge before school. Have to see how things are going. Promise you'll read this over so I can post it when I get back? Then I'll walk with you to school."

"I don't need you to walk with me. Hey, you're going to post it without Gord's permission?"

I glare at her. "Dad approved it. Gord's in charge of building the jump, not advertising it. And I'm the boss. Dad said so."

"Yeah right," she says, rolling her eyes. She picks up the broom and starts sweeping the kitchen.

Gord's not on the half-installed catwalk. I decide to crawl on the pipe beneath it to inspect his latest work. The first few sections of the walk are in place. They look awesome. Rivets, check. Bolts, check.

I run my hand over a brand-new weld. Someday, I'm going to build bridges. Suspension bridges, Bailey bridges, all kinds of bridges. Maybe even bridges with bungee-jump platforms. I'm going to be a great engineer.

My fingertips pass over a joint I can't see. It's behind a steel piece of the trestle. I pause. And I pass my fingers over it again.

Prickles run down my neck. Something's not right. I grip two steel plates for support. Then I twist my body around to see behind them. Sure enough, there's a hairline crack, a tiny gap in the weld.

What do I do? Ask Gord? Or—wait, I have a better idea! I pull my cell phone out and drape my body in an even crazier position. I aim the phone behind the weld and snap a photo. *Oops!* I nearly tumble off trying to get the phone back into my pocket.

"Christopher Bigg!" Gord calls from above me on the catwalk. "What are you doing down there? I swear you're going to fall one of these days. Then everyone will blame me, eh? Your interest in engineering is getting crazy dangerous, kid. Just 'cause your father isn't here doesn't mean you can—"

I catapult myself up to the catwalk. "Sorry, Gord, gotta run. But hey, check out the website today!" And I sprint away toward the peninsula side. I want to get to school early so I can talk to Mr. Roth.

"It's dubious," Mr. Roth says, studying my cell-phone shot. "You're on to something, Chris. You don't want shoddy work on something as important as a bungee-jump platform. Lives are at stake."

"What do I do?"

"Call city hall. Ask for an inspector."

"Will that cost money?"

"No. The permit your dad took out covers that. Also, have your dad confront him. This engineer is working for you guys, after all." He shakes his head. "Seems strange someone with those qualifications would make such a big mistake. But good for you, Chris, for being so sharp."

We're interrupted by my cell phone buzzing.

"Sorry, Mr. Roth." I turn away and put the phone to my ear. "Hey, Gord. What's up?"

"You put stuff about leprosy on the bungee-jump site!"

"Yeah, it's part of the history of the island. So?"

"Chris, you're going to have snoops and looters crawling all over the island, not coming for jumping. And I'm living there!"

"Sorry, Gord, if you don't like what I put on the website. Dad said it was great."

I push *end call* as he starts shouting at me. It's rude, but what's with him? It really isn't any of his business. Why get so upset about a little history?

Anyway, it's time to call an inspector. And order Gord to redo that weld.

Chapter Eight

"School picnic day!" Caitlin says in a singsongy voice, skipping beside me on the way to school.

"Yup. Who'd have thought they'd choose Hospital Island for our spring picnic?" I ask. "But it's good. It's a chance for us to remind them about the bungee-jump opening next week."

Someone at city hall arranged for the inspector after I called. Gord redid the weld on the hairline crack without complaining, and everything's good on the bridge.

"Bungee-jump opening!" Caitlin sings in her annoying voice.

"I wonder why Mrs. Dubin didn't volunteer to come on the picnic as a chaperone," Caitlin says.

"Yeah, well, she didn't need to rage about it to the principal," I reply. "She's really got a thing about no one visiting that place."

"You mean about not disturbing history," Caitlin sings.

"She's a grump," I say. "She chewed me out about my website. Like it's any of her business."

"Well, you got some of the history from her."

"So what? It's our property. And our website."

Caitlin makes a face, wags a finger and lowers her voice to imitate the librarian. "You wrote things people don't need to know! Plus, it's not respectful enough."

"I thought she'd like that I included history in it."

"Chris! Caitlin!" Mr. Roth appears. "Hey, everyone, the Biggs are here! Everyone's got their picnic lunch, right?"

"Yes!" the kids shout, lifting water bottles and knapsacks and such.

"Do we get to go on the bungee rope today?" Tom asks.

"Next week," I respond, drawing myself up proudly. "But you can see it from the picnic place."

A bunch of parents who've volunteered to take us on their boats are waiting for us at the dock. There are six boats in all, enough to take all the sixth-, seventh- and eighth-graders of our tiny school.

"I want to go on the Thompsons' cruiser!"

"Please, can I go on the Smiths' runabout?"

"We get the dinghy!"

"That rowboat's only going to take four!"

"Do we have to wear lifejackets?"

"Hey, stop pushing!"

"Chris," Tom calls out. "Come in our boat!"

"Thanks!" I climb into Tom's parents' eight-passenger ketch and smile at his dad, who's operating it. Mr. Roth and half a dozen kids clamber aboard too. Including Caitlin, Bella and Anya.

On the way across the channel, an eagle flies overhead. Everyone points and starts talking at the same time. Soon we come within view of the pipe bridge. A couple of kids get so excited, they lean over the railings.

"Stand back and settle down!" Tom's dad orders, and they do.

"It's like shiny new!" Tom exclaims. He hasn't seen the pipe since he and I snuck up and crawled along it months ago. His parents grounded him when they found out.

"It's so high," says Bella with big, frightened eyes.

"Is that diving-board thing where we jump from?" Anya asks, pointing to the newly installed platform.

"Of course," Caitlin tells her.

"What if you land in the water?" a tall girl from my grade asks.

"You can't, because the rope stops you before then," I say.

The boat slows, and Mr. Roth leans over the side.

"Craven, good morning. How are you? Catch anything this morning?"

"How could I catch anything with you bunch stirring up the water?" Craven grumbles.

"We're on our annual school picnic," Mr. Roth replies, his voice cheerful. "Join us if you like."

Craven looks confused. "Not on Thorn Island," he rasps.

"Yes, on Hospital Island," Mr. Roth replies, nodding at Tom's dad to carry on to shore. "The Biggs have generously given us permission."

Craven rises in his boat, causing it to rock. "Don't you go there!" he roars.

The younger students cower. The others look from Craven to Mr. Roth to Caitlin and me.

"Don't worry," Mr. Roth says in a polite tone. "We won't disturb anything. And we won't leave any garbage behind. Right, kids? See you later, Craven. Have a good day!"

The boats beach. Kids jump out and run to shore like soldiers on D-Day. They ignore Craven's protests.

"He's not having a very good day, is he?" Mr. Roth says to me, smiling reassuringly. "But we're going to have a super picnic anyway."

The adults keep the kids from wandering into the ruins. Probably just as well, since Craven beaches his boat and keeps watch from the shore. We spread blankets on a rise, and someone pulls out a Frisbee. We toss that around and play some games. Someone points out a family of otters in the water.

"Time to eat!" Mr. Roth finally announces. We pull out our bags of food.

I wander off to eat with my friends. We skip flat stones into the water.

Owooo. A weird voice floats over the picnic area.

"What's that?" Tom asks.

"A kid pretending to be a ghost," I say, ignoring the younger students' scared faces and searching for the source of the sound.

"Mr. Roth," Anya calls out just then. She's standing over us, holding a half-eaten sandwich that smells like tuna. Her face looks pale to me.

"Yes, Anya?"

"I don't feel so good."

"Oh, I'm sorry, Anya. Would you like—"

She bolts away for some bushes. She sprays them with vomit.

"Gross!" Tom exclaims. Other kids cover their mouths, giggle or stare at the poor girl.

"Oh-oh," Mr. Roth says as he and a mom-volunteer hustle over to Anya.

A boat with two adults and Anya leaves early. The rest of the kids try to play Frisbee again, but no one seems into it.

"Anya has leprosy," I hear someone whisper.

I leap up to challenge them. I notice a bunch of kids stampeding for the boats. Not Tom or any of my friends, of course. And the kids leaving seem more excited than scared, like they're thrilled by the drama. But I don't like the way they look back at Caitlin and me.

No way. They don't really think... That is the stupidest rumor anyone could start. But it's not like anyone asks me. And just like that, the annual school picnic is over.

Chapter Nine

"A couple of kids are saying it's your fault that Anya got sick," Tom warns me over lunch the following Monday. "And three other kids are home sick today. *I* know it's stupid. And all of our crowd is sticking up for you. But you should know that everyone is saying you shouldn't have invited the school to a contaminated site."

"It's not a contaminated site!" I say louder than necessary. "Anya's mom even called my mom to say it was the mayonnaise in her sandwich."

"Yeah right. Trying to cover it all up?" says Bella, seated down the table from Tom. "And that island is haunted too. Something was wailing during the picnic."

I shake my head, wanting to laugh, except it's not funny. "You fell for some kid sneaking away and trying to scare us?" I ask. "And there are always a few kids absent for being sick. Anyway, it can take months or years for leprosy to show up—"

Oops, dumb thing to say. Now even my friends are looking at each other like they've got something new to get worried-excited about.

"Leprosy is where your arms and legs fall off!" someone declares as they walk by.

"And you die," says a younger student.

"No one will go anywhere near you."

"There's no cure," someone adds.

"Not true!" I protest. "There is a cure. Has been since 1982."

It seems like everyone has an opinion. Things get loud.

That's when Mr. Roth appears. He must have heard some of the comments. He walks over. He rests his hand on my shoulder.

"Need some scientific clarification here?" He eyes the students at my table and beyond.

I hunch over and stare at my lunch bag.

"Teacher's pet," someone hisses.

Mr. Roth removes his hand and narrows his eyes. "There will be a special assembly later this morning to address some rumors we understand are going around. Don't miss it," he warns. His stern eyes rest on each student.

Just what I need, a spotlight on the whole thing. Oh well. Whatever it takes to put things right before the bungee-jump opening.

I'm headed for the assembly when a hand reaches out from nowhere. It closes around my wrist. It yanks me through a doorway.

Okay, not any doorway. Into the school library. I've never seen Mrs. Dubin look so fierce. She points to a chair. She all but pushes me into it.

"You asked for this," she begins.

"For what?" I ask. What will she do if I bolt? I'm not scared of an old lady, am I?

She puts her face right up to mine. So close that I can see two hairs growing out of a mole on her cheek.

"You woke them up. I warned you, over and over. That island is theirs, no matter what you think. When someone troubles them, they make trouble."

Troubles, trouble. Wow, that's almost poetic. What other crap is going to come out of her mouth before I dash to the assembly? I'm going to get in trouble if I don't attend. That's for sure.

"They didn't like our picnic. Is that it?" I ask. "And they made that girl throw up?"

She picks up a ruler from her desk. For a moment I think she's going to hit me with it. Instead, she taps it on a row of dictionaries. *Tap, tap, tap.*

"They've earned their right to peace, Christopher Bigg. Peace, quiet and respect. Your website messed with that. Your picnic upset them. And the bridge project is really stressing them. Imagine what that stupid ride you're working on will do." The ruler slams down on the desk so hard that I jump.

"It's not a stupid ride. It's a bungee—" *Oh, what's the use?* I'm half tempted to say that the jump won't even take kids onto Hospital Island. The platform simply straddles our peninsula and their—I mean, the island.

I could ask, "Do they tell you all this?" Or, "Who do you think you are, a ghost interpreter?" But I'm not in the mood to go head-to-head with Mrs. Dubin.

My mind flashes back to the picnic. Mr. Roth was polite and respectful to Craven.

"I appreciate the historical information you helped me find, Mrs. Dubin," I say.

The librarian drops the ruler. Her eyebrows shoot upward for a second.

"I'm sorry if you felt I put too much information on the website," I continue. "And I am very sorry the leper children suffered all those years ago. But the bungee jump is going to open. So stop threatening me."

With that I leap up and sprint for the door and some fresh air. Air to evaporate the sweat pouring from my armpits.

In the gym, Mr. Roth is giving a lecture on leprosy. It's almost as good as my report. The principal stands to one side of him. Anya and her mother are on the other side, looking sheepish.

Everyone turns and stares at me. I step through the doorway and head for where Tom and my friends are sitting. I spot Caitlin. Her arms are wrapped around herself like she's cold. Her eyes lock on mine. A smile of relief plays across her face.

"So, as I've explained, it's impossible to get leprosy from visiting Hospital Island. And there has been a cure for this historical disease for a long time. That's thanks to the work of scientists. Finally, as Anya's mother has so kindly explained, her daughter's brief illness had nothing to do with the picnic's location."

There's a ripple of dutiful clapping. The principal and teachers direct us back to our classes. Tom and other guys around me clap me on my shoulders.

"Can't believe anyone believed..."

"Bummer that a couple of stupid people caused..."

"We totally stuck up for you but..."

"No problem," I reply. We head down the bleachers and onto the gym floor.

"Nice website."

"Thanks!"

"So who gets to go first at the bungee-jump opening?"

I laugh as a bunch of students press close to us.

"Me!"

"Me!"
"Me!"
"We'll see," I reply.

Chapter Ten

"It's not the official opening, you know." I'm addressing a crowd of two dozen kids. They've shown up for the bungee jump's first test. We tried to make today's event hush-hush. Lot of good that did.

"Yes, the real opening is next week, if all goes well today," Gord says from beside me.

Next week. I hope Dad can make it. Mom promised to take the afternoon off work. Bummer that she can't be here today.

"But we can watch, can't we?" asks Tom, standing beside eager-looking Bella and Anya.

"Of course," Caitlin says, "but everyone has to stand back behind this gate." The gate opens onto the catwalk. "Except Gord, Chris and Chuck."

"Chuck is the jump master," I explain.

The safety guy smiles and waves at everyone. He's dressed in jeans, a Hospital Island T-shirt and army boots. The T-shirt order arrived yesterday, and the three of us are wearing the first ones out of the box.

Mrs. Dubin will probably kill me when she sees them. They have a ghost figure on them. And she always calls it Thorn Island. But Dad and Gord said my idea was clever.

Over his T-shirt Chuck is wearing a harness with metal rectangles clipped all over it. Dad arranged for him weeks ago. I just had to phone up and say we were finally ready. He's as stoked as I am about the test today.

"Hey, kids." Chuck waves at them. "Yes, normally I make sure jumpers have the gear on right. And that the rope's good. I also tell them when they can leap. But today I'm doing the actual test jump. Next week when we open, I'll be helping all of you!"

"Yeah!"

The kids gape at the metal stuff hanging off his harness. They stare like he's a Martian or a god.

"You three can now come through the gate," Caitlin informs Chuck, Gord and me. Her voice is loud and bossy.

"How come you guys get to go and not us?" demands Tom. I roll my eyes 'cause I've already explained it to him.

"We're not insured for anyone else to be on the pipe bridge till the test jump is completed," Gord tells the crowd.

Gord, Chuck and I walk past Caitlin. I nod to her and turn to wave at my friends. But everyone's eyes are fastened on Chuck, who is walking ahead of me. Gord is behind me.

Caitlin remains where she is to guard the gate. No one's going to get past her easily, I reflect with a smile.

My hands are sweaty on the catwalk's cable railing. I look down through the metal grating my feet are creeping along. Below me is the old pipe. Patched and painted silver, it looks new. But it's the same old pipe I crawled on top of many times. It was dumb doing that without railings, of course—but so fun. I never could handle being inside it like Caitlin can.

I look past the pipe, down at Misty Passage. Waves whipped up by the afternoon breeze dance. Droplets spit into the air. The water's waiting for Chuck to drop down. A brave, flying leap. Then *boing, boing, boing*. I shiver. I'll be doing it next week.

Watching the currents below makes me a little dizzy. So I study the back of Chuck's T-shirt instead. *Everything's going to be fine. The kids will be impressed. Word will spread. Next week's opening will be everything we've waited for.*

The crowd goes quiet as our little parade nears the middle of the bridge. We pause on the platform, which is a metal cage with a gate and wooden "tongue" sticking out over the water.

Chuck steps onto it first. He has already checked and rechecked the rope. It's as thick as my wrist. It's anchored to the cage floor and coiled inside the gate.

"What all does a jump master do?" I ask Chuck.

"I keep a log of the rope's condition. I check wind conditions. I look for objects that could cause problems—telephone wires, boulders. None of those here." He points to a scale. "I have to weigh each jumper. Then I adjust the cord's length for their weight. No one under seventy-five pounds is allowed.

"After someone jumps and stops rebounding, I activate the electric winch. That brings the jumper back up. By then the next jumper is ready."

"I get to operate the winch today," Gord says proudly. He pats the winch machinery. Its cable disappears through a hole in the pipe. "So, Chuck, will you touch the water before the rope stops?"

"No worries. No one's going to touch the water. Almost, but not quite. I've made sure."

Chapter Eleven

“Okay, it’s time,” Chuck says, winking at me.

He pulls on gloves and a helmet. His harness looks like suspenders over his shoulders and a strap around his chest. A giant metal rectangle hangs from where the two meet. He clips the big cord into this.

"Now I'm going to stand where the big red footprints are," Chuck says. He pushes open the little gates. He moves to the end of the platform.

"Go! Go! Go!" the students near Caitlin chant.

She stands with arms out to block them from going onto the catwalk. But they're pressing against her and the gate. They're clapping and getting excited.

"Is your bridge ready?" Chuck teases Gord. "Because my rope system and I are."

Then he steps off the board as casually as if he was walking through a doorway.

Whoosh! He's gone. At the same time, I hear a burst of cheers. I also feel the catwalk floor and platform vibrate.

As Chuck free-falls toward Misty Passage, the students push past Caitlin and the gate for a better view.

The walkway above the pipe shakes. I grip the railing.

"Chuck is rebounding, Gord," I report. "Okay, now he's done rebounding."

Gord pushes the winch button to pull Chuck up. Nothing happens. There is no buzz telling us the machinery is working. Chuck remains dangling over the water.

The kids charge toward us. Some are screaming. Some have fallen onto the catwalk. They're trampling over each other. Any more panic and someone is bound to fall off the bridge.

"What should I do, Gord?" I ask, my pulse throbbing.

"Run to the Hospital Island end, Chris. Before the kids get here. Then crawl into the pipe. In the middle, right below us, there's a cord for the winch. It must have come loose. Plug it in."

"Okay."

Gord turns to the kids and shouts, "Freeze! Now!"

"Is Chuck stuck?" I hear Caitlin's voice behind the kids.

I don't hear Gord's reply. I'm too busy sprinting along the catwalk, away from the pack.

Get to the end of the pipe. Fast. That's the easy part. On the Hospital Island side, I step onto solid ground. Then I spin around. I know the combination to open the new locked door on the pipe's end.

I know where Gord put the electrical outlet inside the pipe. I saw it on the plans. I watched him crawl in to install it. He put it inside to protect it from weather, he told me. The vibrations on the catwalk must have disconnected the cord.

Mr. Roth would say that's bad planning. But all that matters right now is that Chuck is helpless till I reach that outlet. And seeing him hanging there could make the kids panic more.

Crawl inside the pipe! I order myself. But my knees refuse to cooperate.

My fear of small, dark spaces comes spiraling down and crushes me. I collapse into a useless heap. My chin is on the grass just inches from the pipe entrance. My hands are clutching my head. I try, but I just can't make myself enter that dark space. Not even to save Chuck.

After several minutes of misery, I hear a buzz and a rumble. I look toward the water and see Chuck traveling upward. Through the air, courtesy of the winch. He's smiling with relief.

The screaming on the bridge has stopped. But a noise just inside my end of the pipe draws my eyes into the darkness. The next thing I know, Caitlin leaps out and throws her arms around my neck. I topple backward.

Caitlin's frightened, sweaty face looks into mine as she hugs me tightly.

"I was so, so scared," she says. "I came through the pipe to help you. From the other side. Gord said you were plugging in the cord that got loose. When I didn't see you there, I did it. Are you okay? Will Chuck be okay? The kids were horrible. They pushed each other. They knocked me down. Is everyone going to be all right?"

Chapter Twelve

"No one was hurt badly," I tell Dad over the phone. "A couple of kids got scrapes and bruises."

Mom is beside me. She's replacing a bandage on Caitlin's shoulder, where the edge of the hatch that hangs down from the middle of the pipe scraped her on her way to the electrical outlet. The outlet I should have gotten to first.

We're on speaker phone so we can all chat.

"The kids panicked when the catwalk started to vibrate," I add.

"They weren't supposed to be on the catwalk! They pushed right past me!" Caitlin adds.

"Is Chuck okay?" Dad asks.

"Yeah, Gord pulled Chuck up as soon as Caitlin plugged the cord in. Chuck was spooked, but he says it was a problem with Gord's plans. Nothing to do with the rope itself."

"And what does Gord say?"

"That it was just the winch's cord pulling out. He says it was no big deal."

"No big deal?" Mom and Dad echo in stunned tones.

"But Mr. Roth told me something."

"What did he tell you, son?"

"That no qualified engineer would've put the outlet inside the pipe like that. Too inaccessible. That it should be outside and waterproofed. He says Gord seems sloppy. But he says it won't cost much to change it so that it's right."

"Hmmm," is all Dad says.

"Can you send us money to move the outlet, Dad?" I ask. "Otherwise people will think we have a real problem."

"They already do," Caitlin mutters.

"What are you saying, Caitlin?" Dad asks.

"They say the bridge is haunted," Caitlin blurts out. "That the leper children won't let us bungee-jump there. That there were ghost howls on the island when it happened."

Dad laughs so loudly I have to back away from the phone. "That's a good one. Way better than a structural problem."

Caitlin frowns. Mom pats her on the head. My sister says nothing more.

"Well, I'll send what I can," Dad says. "Better get that outlet moved and the bridge inspected again."

At school, the kids are divided into two groups. There are those who believe the island and bridge are haunted. And the rest make fun of them. Luckily, most of the kids who whisper about ghosts are too young to go on the bungee jump anyway. They are under the required seventy-five pounds.

"Still opening next week?" Tom asks as he walks down the hall with his arms full of books.

I hedge. "Maybe two weeks. I can let you be the first to jump, if you like."

"Awesome! Do I get a Hospital Island T-shirt too?"

I grin. "Twenty bucks. And a promise to never wear it into the school library."

We both laugh, since he knows all about Mrs. Dubin and her thing for *respectful history*.

"What're you doing your science paper on this week?" Tom asks me.

I squirm. "Claustrophobia. That's a fear of small spaces."

"Oh. That's science?"

"Well, scientists have studied it and looked for cures. Mr. Roth said it was okay. Have you picked a topic yet?"

"Yes! Bungee-jump engineering!"

"Cool! Gord's got books in his trailer if you need to borrow any."

"I've been up to the bridge a couple of times. Hoping to talk with him. But he's never there. Always on the island with that metal detector. Walking back and forth, back and forth."

I sigh. "Well, I guess he's allowed to do that on breaks."

"Think he's looking for the gold?"

"What gold?"

"You know, the gold the doctor hid."

"That's just a dumb story, Tom. And it wasn't gold. Cash, people say. In a metal box."

Tom shakes his head. "Why else would he spend all that time with a metal detector? Maybe he'll find the box and get rich."

"He's not going to get rich from a couple of coins that don't even exist!" I say it forcefully, because I suddenly wonder if Tom is right. Even if the money box is a made-up story, Gord might believe it. That may explain why he's not getting enough work done. Or being sloppy when he does do it. I grit my teeth and decide to confront him.

"Chris!" It's Mr. Roth.

Tom gives me a thumbs-up and disappears.

"Hi, Mr. Roth."

"So, I went up to the pipe bridge like you asked."

"Already?" I hope he didn't tell Gord I sent him.

"Your engineer wasn't around, so I went looking around without permission."

"Fine with me."

"I gave the new outlet and cable a close inspection."

"Yeah?" The city-hall inspector approved it already, but I figured a second pair of eyes wouldn't hurt.

"It's all good now. Too bad he didn't do it right the first time."

"So it's not haunted," I say, trying to joke.

He smiles. "All phenomena can be explained by science."

I nod slowly. "Even claustrophobia?"

"Tell me why you ask that."

Since no one is within earshot, I spill the whole story. About how I've never been able to crawl inside the pipe. About how I failed everyone during the bungee-test crisis. How Chuck might have been hanging for way longer if not for Caitlin.

He nods all the time I'm talking. He doesn't look at me like he feels sorry for me. He doesn't tell me I'm a chicken.

"All phenomena can be explained," he repeats.

I wait.

"Everyone is born with survival instincts, Chris. Some small, dark spaces can make people suffocate—die for lack of air. So it's natural to be cautious. It's a good reaction. Claustrophobic people—6 percent of the population—just have that instinct stronger than the rest of us. They usually get it from an experience when they were young."

"I got trapped in a closet when I was little," I admit. "Is there a cure?"

"Actually, there are two cures. One is talking yourself out of it. Making your brave, logical voice louder than the scared one. The second is making yourself go into a small, dark space for a really short time. Then slightly longer. Then slightly longer. Till you aren't scared anymore."

I feel released from a weight of shame and misery.

"You'll learn more when you work on your report," he adds, winking. "Good luck, Chris."

"Thanks, Mr. Roth. Tell the kids who are scared of ghosts too, okay?"

"Tell them what?"

"That all phenomena can be explained. And that science is—well, cool!"

He laughs as he walks down the hall.

Chapter Thirteen

After school, Caitlin and I climb up the bluff to the bridge.

"Hey, Gord and Chuck!" I say.

"Hey," they reply. Both have long faces.

"Something wrong?"

"Your dad called," Gord says. "Said he can't pay either of us after next week. He got laid off."

"Oh." I hang my head, even though it means maybe he'll come home. Caitlin's hand goes to her mouth.

"So if we don't open next week, it's all over. Unless we work for free. Which we don't," Gord adds firmly. Chuck nods.

"Can you finish it and open by next week?" I ask, my stomach tightening.

"Well, I've finished relocating the electrics. The inspectors have okayed everything. And Chuck has done a second test jump. He needs someone your size to do one too. Then we have cleanup to tackle. And signs to put up. If we work really, really hard, then yes, it's possible."

"I'll help!" Caitlin says quickly. "Maybe Mom too."

Gord stands and nods. "Okay. Caitlin, can you load the empty paint cans into that truck over there? And after your jump, Chris, can you help clear that pile of old girders down the bluff?"

"You bet!" says Caitlin, scampering away.

"For sure," I promise. Then I follow Chuck to the platform and let him weigh me.

"It's your big moment, Chris," he says, giving me a smile that boosts my confidence.

I tug on the gloves he hands me. He adjusts the helmet's chinstrap. He helps me into the harness. It fits snugly around my shoulders and waist. Then he lifts the heavy bungee rope and clips it onto the harness's metal rectangle.

"Red footprints," I say before he points. I'm shaking slightly as I shuffle toward them. I peer over the toes of my shoes to the water far below. I'm leaping down *there*? Tom's dad has positioned his ketch near shore, ready to help in an emergency.

"Ready when you are, Chris," Chuck declares.

My mouth is dry. My hands inside the gloves are moist. My heart is doing flip-flops from stomach to throat. My knees are threatening to buckle. I crack a smile and draw in a deep breath. I tell myself it's just the high diving board at school.

"Here goes nothing," I say. As I step off the platform, it feels like I'm leaping out of an airplane door.

Whoosh! I'm free-falling toward sparkling water. The descent sucks the air out of my lungs. My entire body tingles as it drops. The channel rushes up. For a split second I think I'm going to land right in it. Then my plunge slows. The cord stretches, stretches, stretches. Will it stop me in time?

Gently, it reaches its maximum stretchiness. Teasingly, it halts just before my shoes would touch water.

It yanks me back up. Up, up, up as Misty Passage grows smaller and smaller. And then, like a roller-coaster rider who has reached the top of an arch, I'm free-falling again. Screaming in delight this time.

"Whoopee! Yeaaaaaah!"

Three times, four times, the rope rebounds. Each time a little less distance. And then it's all played out.

I hang limply. A puppet on a string. What if the device doesn't pull me up? I could—

I am being lifted gently away from the water. It is like a ski lift or a glass elevator. The view is stunning. Have I ever really appreciated it before? The peninsula, our farm, the island. It's all surrounded by quiet, tranquil water. Birds soar overhead. Did the peace and natural beauty help the leper kids?

The elevator keeps going up, up, up. Fifteen floors' worth. Did I really just fall all this way in a split second? The buzz in my body lingers. It was *awesome*. I want to do it again. I want everyone within a hundred miles to do it. I want opening day to be super incredibly amazing!

"Perfect," Chuck says with a big grin as my feet touch the platform. He unhooks me.

"Next?" he says kiddingly to Gord.

"Don't look at me!" Gord laughs. "Too much work to do."

I've barely shed the harness when I head down the catwalk to help with the cleanup. I'll get up early tomorrow and do more work before school. I'll be here minutes after school every day. I'll grab Tom and other friends to help. We're going to make the deadline! No one and nothing—neither ghosts nor money problems—are going to stop us.

Chapter Fourteen

"Lucky it's a full moon," I say.

The trees, the channel and the path are bathed in eerie white. Caitlin and I have snuck out of the house. Mom's sleeping. We're headed up the bluff.

"So Mr. Roth told you exactly all the things to look at?"

"Yup, I've got a checklist." The list from Mr. Roth left nothing out.

It included bringing a second harness that just arrived. I'm wearing that for fun. "Couldn't do an inspection while Gord was there this afternoon. We're making triple sure everything's good to go for tomorrow."

"Shhh. What's that?" I hold up my hand to halt my sister. We're nearing the bridge. I'm sure I hear footfalls.

Creak.

"That's the door to the pipe, isn't it?" Caitlin whispers. "Gord must've forgotten to lock it. Or someone has broken in."

"Someone has gone in there? They're trying to hide. And they might have been messing with the mechanics!"

Owoooo!

"What's that?" Caitlin asks in a panicked voice.

"Someone trying to scare us," I say. "A fake ghost we're going to catch."

I put my flashlight on full beam and sprint toward the pipe.

"Wait for me!" Caitlin cries.

I grab her hand. When we get there, sure enough, the door's unlocked and ajar.

"We're going in!" I say. *I am not afraid.* I've been working on the "cures" for claustrophobia that Mr. Roth told me about. *It's just a pipe. Must catch this person.*

We crawl along inside the pipe. My flashlight beam cuts through the dark. We stop and listen.

Bang! Click!

"The door!" Caitlin screams. "Someone shut it behind us!"

Owoooo! The shriek comes from outside the pipe. It's more than one voice. Soon there are heavy footfalls above us. On the catwalk.

My chest tightens. I'm gasping for breath. I force myself to breathe slowly and concentrate.

Before, there were a few holes in the pipe. Places I could've seen out. Places

I could have punched my way through. But Gord and I patched all of them.

"We have to get to the door on the far end," Caitlin says. I feel her shivering beside me.

"There's also the middle hatch," I say. The one Caitlin always bumps her head on. The one I always climbed over on my way to the other side.

"That has always been stuck," Caitlin says.

"Well, I have some tools with me." Lucky that Mr. Roth told me to bring some.

We crawl to the hatch. Caitlin holds the flashlight. I chip away with my crowbar and screwdriver.

"Watch out!" Caitlin screams.

I jump back just in time. The rusty bottom half of the hatch falls heavily.

"Huh?" I mumble. There's a rusty box at my feet. Hidden inside the hatch for who knows how many years.

Caitlin grabs my screwdriver and pries it open.

"*Whoa!*" We stare as our beam reveals hundreds of coins and dollar bills.

"The cash box!" we say at the same time.

"Hello?" comes a voice from above us. "Who's in there?"

"Gord!" we shout in relief. "We're trapped in the pipe! Can you get the top of the hatch open?"

He pries open the hatch, grunting. I've never been so happy to feel night air against my face. The moon lights up the box in our hands.

"What in heaven's name are you doing in there? And at this time of night? What's that?" he asks while lowering an arm to help Caitlin up first.

"An old box full of money!" Caitlin says excitedly. "Maybe the one that the doctor—"

"Seriously?" he interrupts. He releases her hand to grab the box and lifts it up to his chest. "Let me take care of this, kids. I'll get it to the proper authorities."

"Hey!" Caitlin shouts as he disappears. We hear his footfalls on the catwalk, racing toward Hospital Island.

Shock and silence reign between us. The moon slides behind a cloud.

"He's coming back, right?" my sister asks in a small voice.

"I don't know," I say, thoughts tumbling over one another. "But either way, we can get out now."

And yet, as I lower cupped hands to give her a leg up, the top of the hatch door crashes down with startling force.

"Oh no!" Caitlin cries out.

"Don't worry," I reassure her between gritted teeth. "I'll get it open again."

"But why didn't Gord help us out?" Caitlin asks, a tremor in her voice.

"Maybe he doesn't care about us," I say. "I'm thinking he was after that money all along."

I grab thc crowbar and slam it against the hatch door. "The metal detector. The sloppy work. The way he told Dad he'd work for less than other engineers. Maybe he never really cared about the bungee jump or—"

"—us," Caitlin finishes for me. "We have to get the hatch open again. Or run for the far door."

"I'll—get—this—open." I apply one tool after another. Finally, I get some lift. I push with all my strength. At first it resists. Then it flies open so fast I lose my balance. I topple into Caitlin. But four strong arms reach in and lift the two of us out.

The next thing I know, we're out of the pipe and on the catwalk. Right beside the platform. Between Mrs. Dubin and Craven. The moon behind them has turned them into spooky silhouettes.

Chapter Fifteen

"Th-th-thank you," Caitlin stutters, gawking at our rescuers.

"We told you and told you," Mrs. Dubin says, her hold on my wrist so tight that it hurts. "Okay, tie them up, son."

"You bet, Mom," says Craven.

Mom? Craven is Mrs. Dubin's *son*? Whoa, no one ever told me that. Does anyone even know? I try to yank my hand away to run, but Craven is bigger and faster. In seconds, he has Caitlin and me bound together midbody—Caitlin's back to my chest—with a rope he was carrying. He tosses us roughly to the floor of the platform. Caitlin cries out. The back of my head hits the platform. My back ends up arched painfully over the hard coil of bungee rope. We're tied tightly together, but at least our hands are free.

Twisting my head, I see the cash box beside Mrs. Dubin's pointy black boots.

"Where's Gord?" I ask, trying to sound calm.

"Craven took care of him," the librarian says with an ominous smile. "He was greedy and conniving, your engineer."

"You took the box from him," I say. Doesn't that make *them* greedy and conniving? "So the doctor really did take money from the leper kids."

"No one will ever prove that," Mrs. Dubin says, leaning down and putting her face in mine. "My mother and father gave everything for those kids. My father even gave his life. Yes, the doctor and nurse. My parents."

Caitlin and I are speechless.

"So you've been searching for the box all these years?" I say. "Trying to scare people off so you'd find it before them?"

"Wrong. Keeping people away to let the innocent souls and my father rest in peace," she says. "With no smudged reputation."

In other words, she didn't want anyone to find it. If they did, they'd know her father had been stealing. It occurs to me for the first time that she might intend to kill Caitlin and me.

I may not be able to struggle up, but the old lady can't see what my hands are doing behind my back. I maneuver them to grasp the bungee rope.

"You slammed the board down on the hot tub when Caitlin was in it?" I ask.

"That was me," Craven says proudly.

"And wailed during the picnic and earlier tonight?"

"That was me," Craven says proudly again.

"And trapped us in the pipe just now?"

"Both of us," Mrs. Dubin replies curtly.

"But you never knew the doctor hid the box in the hatch? Not before we found it tonight?"

"What box?" Mrs. Dubin roars. She pushes through the gate and stands on the red footprints. She opens the box and lifts out a fistful of money.

So she got the box away from Gord before he could get the money.

She lets coins and paper money drop from her fingers. Then she tips the entire contents out. Money fills the air. It rains down to Misty Passage. To sink forever. Finally, she heaves the empty box off the bridge.

"Oh!" Caitlin exclaims.

"Those stories of a box were nothing but nasty rumors," she declares.

She never wanted the money. She just wanted people to admire her father.

She comes back through the gate and steps over us. She stands on the platform, arms crossed. "My father didn't deserve nasty rumors."

"Did he fall or commit suicide?" I dare to ask. I'm busy grasping the bungee rope's metal rectangle.

Mrs. Dubin kicks me with one of her pointed boots, prompting Caitlin to scream. The kick shoves us closer to the gate.

She bends down again to put her ugly face beside mine. Her breath smells sour. "He fell during a delirious fever," she says. "So sad. He gave his life for the hospital."

"Then your mother ran away and had you," I say. Behind my back, I quietly click the bungee clip to my harness.

"Your interest in history is admirable," she says. "But you went too far. Craven, it's time."

She turns and stomps back to the catwalk. Caitlin shuts her eyes. I wince as Craven's big body looms over us. "Have a nice fall," he says and laughs.

"I've got you!" I whisper to my sister. And I wrap my arms around her with all my strength.

His kick would impress a professional football scout. We skid under the platform gate and over the red footprints. We fly off the board. Caitlin's scream deafens me. Her small hands are clenched around my wrists.

"One thousand, two thousand, three—" I count. *Boing!* Caitlin screams again.

I smile. We're traveling up, up, up. And down. A couple of rebounds and we're hanging limply, no movement. But what if Craven or his mother cuts the rope from above?

Swish, swish. Out of the darkness, Craven's rowboat comes at us. *No way.* He didn't have time to run down and get in it already.

Swish, swish. A crumpled-up man is working the oars. Cursing like he's in pain.

He reaches us. He positions the boat so that we're dangling over it. He stands and lifts a knife. Caitlin opens her mouth, but a third scream doesn't come.

"Don't cut it!" I order Gord. "Unhook it instead. Or the rope will be damaged for tomorrow."

His face is bloodied where Craven's fist landed. He's cradling a rib with one curled-up hand.

"Smart thinking, Chris," he says. He eases our weight onto his shoulders for a second. Then unclips us. *Thwack.* We fall into the boat, still tied up.

"Ouch," Caitlin says.

"Sorry, Caitlin," Gord says as he uses his knife to slice Craven's ropes off us. We're free!

"How'd you—?" he starts to ask.

"Was wearing the new harness. Slipped the bungee rope onto it when they weren't looking," I say.

"So glad you're okay," he says, leaning forward to squeeze our shoulders as we sit up. "I'm sorry," he adds. "I wanted that cash box so badly. I didn't think it would hurt anyone to poke around and—"

"They tried to kill us," I say, looking up at thc bridge.

"I know. And they beat me to a pulp," he says, lifting his torn shirt to point at bruises. "But I got myself to

Craven's boat. I called the police on my cell. And I was hoping I could rescue you if they..."

Caitlin faces Gord. "You left us without helping us out of the hatch," she says.

Gord hangs his head. "I'm sorry. I just wanted the box. I only meant to delay you for a few minutes. I didn't know what those two were up to."

"Why were you up there?"

"I came up when I saw flashlight beams. I heard the pipe door slam. I went on the catwalk, looking. Then I heard you."

"And as you ran off with the box, they caught you," I say.

"Yes," he says. "After they beat me up, I saw them go back onto the catwalk. And I saw them throw the money into the water." He stares at the black water around us, a tragic look on his face.

The sound of police-car sirens shatters the night's quiet. They're heading up the peninsula toward the bridge. Meanwhile, a police boat speeds up the channel. It beaches on Hospital Island. Police dogs bark excitedly as they jump to shore.

"Are you a real engineer, Gord?" I ask.

He takes the oars and studies the floor of the boat. "No, Chris. I'm a draftsman and contractor. I studied to be an engineer but flunked the exam. I faked some papers when I heard your dad was looking for someone. I'm sorry. You'll turn me in, eh?"

"Not till after the opening tomorrow," I reply.

Caitlin looks surprised, then smiles.

Gord winks and grins. Then he rows us to the police boat.

Chapter Sixteen

"Yahoo!" screams Tom as he drops off the platform.

"That's an enthusiastic one," Chuck says, grinning at me. "Okay, Gord, winch Tom up," he says a few minutes later.

"I'm next!" insists Caitlin. "Can I go upside down?"

"If you're brave enough," Chuck says.

"And I go after Caitlin, right?" comes a deep voice.

I spin around. I envelop Dad in a bear hug. "You made it, Dad!"

"Wouldn't miss it for anything," he says. His arms reach out to hug Caitlin and me. Mom is behind him, smiling.

"You did it, Chris. You really did it," Dad says.

"Caitlin helped," I say.

"Yeah, and I'm about to go on the jump upside down!" she enthuses.

"That's my girl," Dad says with a chuckle. "I swear you've grown in the last few weeks."

"Look at the lineup," Mom says, beaming. "We've taken in a mountain of money."

"And this is only the first day," Gord says, smiling wide.

I high-five him.

"Chris!" Mr. Roth has worked his way up in line. "I'm so proud of you!"

"Thanks for your help," I say at the same time as Dad, and we laugh. As Dad shakes hands with my science teacher, Mom watches Chuck weigh Caitlin.

"Did you hear they're going to hire a new librarian?" she asks us.

"Yeah. A younger one, I hope." I chuckle. "And you know what I'm going to ask the new one?"

"What, dear?"

"To set up a special section in the library about Hospital Island. History and posters that honor the leper kids. And the people who took care of them."

Mom draws me into a hug. "And I hear you and Caitlin have rounded up a bunch of kids to clean up the island."

"Yeah. Clear the garbage out. Cut the grass. Put up some plaques. Maybe offer tours."

"Tours?" Mom raises her eyebrows.

"For donations. The money will go to leprosy projects around the world."

"There are still leper colonies? Even though there's a cure?" she asks.

"There are still kids with leprosy who need help. Even though there's a cure. And someday, when I'm an engineer, I'm going to build hospitals."

"Hospitals? That's my boy!" Dad rejoins the conversation.

"With a tower on the children's wing that has a bungee jump," Caitlin teases.

"Now that would be interesting," Mom says.

"One of a kind," Dad says.

"Go for it." Gord laughs.

"Oh, go jump off a bridge," I tell them all with a grin.

"Just waiting our turn," Dad says.

Acknowledgments

Special thanks to engineer Tony Kavelaars and contractor Bruce Richmond for their patient consultation. Gratitude to Melanie Jeffs, Liz Kemp, Tanya Trafford and the rest of the Orca Book team. Also a shout-out to Colin Thomas, Silvana Bevilacqua, my husband Steve Withers, my literary agent Lynn Bennett and the members of my writing group: David Burrowes, Leanne Dyck and Ben Bergman. And, finally, thanks to my teen readers, Malcolm Scruggs, Bella and Anya.

Award-winning author Pam Withers has written seventeen bestselling sports and adventure books for teens, including two Orca Currents titles: *Camp Wild* and *Daredevil Club*. Pam is a former outdoor guide, journalist, editor and associate publisher. She lives in Vancouver, British Columbia, with her husband and tours North America extensively. For more information, visit www.pamwithers.com.